Theo's Golden
Adventures

CHAPTER 1:
THE BIG FLUFFY ADVENTURER

Meet "THEO", short name for THEODORE.

Theo is no ordinary dog. Sure, he's big, fluffy, and golden, like a walking pillow, but beneath all that soft fur, he's a whirlwind of energy and mischief!

Every morning, when the sun peeks through the windows, Theo is ready to start the day with a bounce and a wiggle.

He dashes around the house like a golden tornado, looking for something exciting to do—and if excitement isn't happening fast enough, HE'LL MAKE IT HAPPEN!

"IAN! Where are you?" Theo seems to ask as his nose open his best friend's bedroom door. Ian is an 8-year-old boy with an adventurous spirit, and Theo is his partner in all things mischievous.

"Down here, **THEO!**" Ian's voice echoes from the kitchen, where his mom, **LAURA**, is making breakfast.

Theo charges down the stairs with his paws thundering like a stampede.

In his rush to greet Ian, he skids across the floor, sliding right into the kitchen table. BANG!

"THEO!" Laura laughs, shaking her head. "You're going to break something one of these days!"

Theo's tongue lolls out in a goofy smile. He might have knocked a few things over, but how could anyone be mad at such a lovable GOOF?

CHAPTER 2:
THE SOCCER BALL DISASTER

One bright and SUNNY afternoon, Ian was thrilled to practice his soccer skills in the backyard, his new soccer ball gleamed in the sun as he kicked it across the yard, aiming for a perfect SHOT!.

Theo ever curious and eager for ACTION spotted the ball and leaped into the fray.

His big fluffy paws batted the ball with glee before
Ian could even BLINK...

Theo's powerful jaws had deflated IT with a loud POP!

The soccer ball lay crumpled on the grass, its air hissing out like a slowly deflating balloon, Theo looked up and Ian with a cheeky grin, his eyes dancing with playful innocence.

The Deflated BALL

Theo's GRIN

Ian and Laura burst into laughter unable to stay mad at Theo's delightful MISCHIEF, Theo had a way of turning every game into an adventure even it if meant sacrificing a soccer BALL or TWO.

CHAPTER 3:
THE GREAT FORT COLLAPSE

One afternoon, Ian had a brilliant IDEA to build a fort in the living room. He draped blankets over chairs, stacked pillows, and created a cozy hideaway.

Theo watched with intense curiosity, his TAIL wagging so fast it looked like it might take off. When the fort was finally finished, IAN crawled inside to test its coziness.

Theo, never one to be left out of the FUN, squeezed his BIG, fluffy body into the fort as well. The fort, now packed with Theo and Ian, was filled with laughter and happy barks.

But Theo's enthusiasm was too much for the fort's delicate structure. With one playful BITE, Theo chewed through a blanket, causing the fort to collapse in a pile of "fluffy CHAOS".

Ian and Laura couldn't stop laughing at the sight of THEO, tangled in blankets and pillows, looking like the happiest DOG in the world.

Theo's PLAYFUL antics always turned even the simplest activities into joyful, unforgettable moments.

CHAPTER 4:
THE TOY DESTROYER

Theo has a peculiar habit when it comes to toys—especially BALLS. While most dogs love to chase and retrieve them, Theo has his OWN unique take on the game. He doesn't fetch the ball and bring it back like a regular retriever. NO!, Theo thinks it's far more fun to steal the ball, run off with it, and then, well... destroy IT.

"READY, Theo?" Ian holds a bright orange ball in his hand, his eyes gleaming with excitement. He winds up and throws it across the yard.

Most dogs would dash after it and happily bring it back, but Theo? Oh, no. NOT Theo.

With a burst of SPEED, Theo races across the yard, grabs the ball in his mouth, and instead of coming back to Ian, he zooms in the opposite direction.

"Theo, no!" Ian shouts, but it's already TOO LATE.

Theo drops the ball between his PAWS, gives it a couple of good chomps, and within seconds, the squeaky toy is no more.

Ian sighs. "That was my last ball, THEO."

Theo sits proudly over his "prize," looking pleased with himself.

Laura chuckles from the porch. "Looks like someone has a new nickname—"Theo the Toy Destroyer!"

Theo doesn't mind his new TITLE. To him, it just means he's really GOOD at his job.

CHAPTER 5:
STICK CHEWING CHAMPION

If there's one thing Theo loves more than toys, it's STICKS. Big sticks, small sticks, twigs—it doesn't matter. If it's made of wood, Theo will find it and chew it. Chewing sticks is one of Theo's favorite HOBBIES, and he takes it very seriously.

ONE afternoon, Theo and Ian are out in the park. Ian is running ahead, searching for bugs, when Theo suddenly stops. His nose twitches in the air—there's a stick nearby, and it's calling **HIS** name.

With a mighty leap, Theo bounds over to a large fallen branch. It's nearly as BIG as he is, but that doesn't deter him one BIT.

Theo lays down with the stick between his paws and begins his favorite task—CHEWING IT to bits. Bits of bark fly everywhere as Theo gnaws away, completely in his element.

Ian watches while shaking his head. "You're like a beaver in DISGUISE, Theo."

But Theo doesn't mind being compared to a beaver. After all, he's the Stick Chewing CHAMPION of the world—or at least of the park.

CHAPTER 6:
THEO'S GOLDEN GREETING

Theo had a special TALENT—he was the most enthusiastic greeter anyone could ever meet. Whether it was friends, family, or even the mailman, Theo greeted them all with the same level of excitement: over-the-top and full of LOVE.

Whenever the doorbell rang, it was like a race to see who could reach the door first.

 It was always Theo.

His usual routine as soon as Theo's heard a door involved his ears perked up, and his tail started wagging furiously, as if he had been waiting for these moments ALL DAY long.

"Calm DOWN, Theo," Laura said every time, trying to hold him back as she opened the door. But there was no stopping him. The moment a door creaked OPEN; Theo shot out like a cannonball.

Theo's tail wagging always left his golden FUR flying everywhere. Within seconds, everyone's clothes would be covered in a thick layer of Theo's FLUFFY hair—almost like they had been hugged by a furry tornado.

Theo also loves showering everyone with slobbery KISSES. No one could escape the enthusiastic face licks, and trying to dodge them only seemed to fuel HIS energy.

He loves nibbling at everything, including hands and clothes, a gesture that was part affection and part mischief. His EYES sparkle with excitement, practically begging for MORE attention...which he receives all the time.

"THAT is a full Theo EXPERIENCE!"

No **ONE** ever left the house without a little bit of Theo on them—whether it was fur, slobber, or just the memory of his goofy, lovable greeting.

CHAPTER 7:
THE CUDDLE MONSTER

Despite his wild antics, Theo has a SOFT side, too. When the day's adventures are over, and Ian is curled up on the couch, Theo turns into the biggest, fluffiest cuddle monster you've ever SEEN.

He'll nudge his way onto the couch, plop his big golden body right next to IAN, and lay his head on Ian's lap. Theo's fur is so soft, it feels like a WARM blanket.

But, as much as Theo loves to cuddle, there's a little trick to it. Just when you think you're in for a peaceful snuggle session, Theo will start gently nibbling on your HAND.

"Theo! Stop... that tickles!" IAN giggles, trying to pull his hand away.

Theo's eyes twinkle with MISCHIEF. He knows exactly what he's doing—exchanging cuddles for a little playful nibbling. And while IAN can't help but laugh, he secretly LOVES it. After all, that's just Theo being THEO.

Theo's life is FULL of adventure, FUN, and LOVE, and no matter how many toys he destroys or sticks he chews, Ian and Laura wouldn't trade him for anything in the WORLD. Because at the end of the day, Theo's the best goofy, lovable, and mischievous DOG anyone could ever have.

What will Theo's NEXT adventure BE?

So, IF you even meet a GOLDEN retriever with a sparkling golden coat and a knack for mischief, you might just be LUCKY enough to meet THEO- the terrific dog who made "Everyday an Adventure and Everyday A Memory to Treasure".

THE END

Picture of the real Theo who inspired THIS book

Made in United States
Orlando, FL
09 April 2025

60318533R00021